SHINY SNOW MACHINES

KINGFISHER
LONDON & NEW YORK

Text copyright © Tony Mitton 2022
Illustrations copyright © Ant Parker 2022
Designed by Anthony Hannant (LittleRedAnt)

Published in the United States by Kingfisher,
120 Broadway, New York, NY 10271
Kingfisher is an imprint of Macmillan Children's Books, London.
Distributed in the U.S. and Canada by Macmillan, 120 Broadway, New York, NY 10271

LIBRARY OF CONGRESS CATALOGING-IN-PUBLICATION DATA HAS BEEN APPLIED FOR

ISBN 978-0-7534-7839-4

Kingfisher books are available for special promotions and premiums. For details contact:
Special Markets Department, Macmillan, 120 Broadway, New York, NY 10271

For more information, please visit
www.kingfisherbooks.com

Printed in China
9 8 7 6 5 4 3 2 1
1TR/0722/WKT/UG/128MA

EU representative: 1st Floor, The Liffey Trust Centre,
117-126 Sheriff Street Upper, Dublin 1 D01 YC43

SHINY SNOW MACHINES

Tony Mitton
and Ant Parker

KINGFISHER
LONDON & NEW YORK

Sledding's very popular,
and yet, who would have thought

dog-sledding through the ice and snow
would be a tourist sport?

For skating rinks we need to have
a smooth and perfect ice.

Resurfacers like this
can make it really oh so nice!

Snow cannons used by ski resorts
can actually make snow.

When it's good and ready—
Whoosh! Watch it blow!

Ski lifts are amazing.
They take you to the top.

When they reach the summit,
quite simply—off you hop!

Ice can be a problem
if it settles on a plane.

Thank goodness for de-icers
that can help it fly again.

When Arctic seas are frozen
with ice that's hard to crack

a boat for breaking ice, like this,
really has the knack.

Snowmobiles are awesome
for riding over snow.

When you need to hurry
that's the way to go!

Ice road trucking's dangerous.
A driver must be tough.

The weather's cold. It's freezing.
The road is hard and rough.

Snow planes zip across the snow.
They make it look such fun.

Here's a happy mailman
doing the postal run.

Snow machines can pump out snow
in weather of all sorts.

They really come in handy
when planning winter sports.

Ice Resurfacer bits

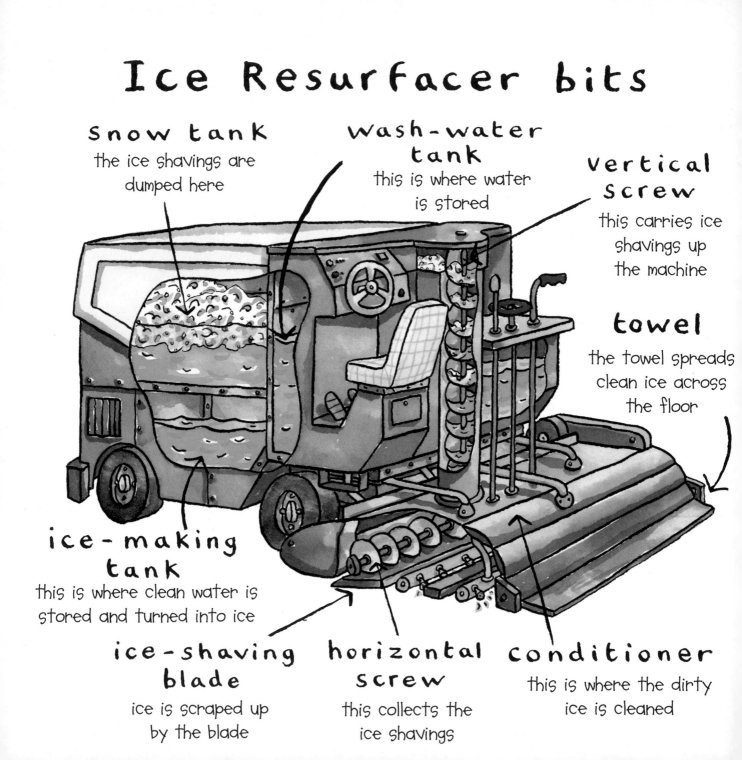

snow tank
the ice shavings are dumped here

wash-water tank
this is where water is stored

vertical screw
this carries ice shavings up the machine

towel
the towel spreads clean ice across the floor

ice-making tank
this is where clean water is stored and turned into ice

ice-shaving blade
ice is scraped up by the blade

horizontal screw
this collects the ice shavings

conditioner
this is where the dirty ice is cleaned

Look out for these **AMAZING** books by Tony Mitton and Ant Parker!

Collect all the **AMAZING MACHINES** picture story books:

Or find your favorites in the **BIG TRUCKLOAD OF FUN—**
the perfect gift for little ones:

Contains 14 Amazing Machines picture story books